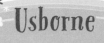

A Sticker Dolly Story
Snow Puppy

D1240582

Zanna Davidson

Illustrated by Katie Wood
Cover illustration by Antonia Miller

Use the stickers to dress the Dolls on the 'Meet the Dolls' pages

Meet the
Animal Rescue Dolls

Amelia, Zoe and Jack are the 'Animal Rescue Dolls'. They look after the animals that live on the Wild Isle, helping animals in trouble and caring for any that are injured.

Amelia

has a special bond with dogs and rabbits. She adores having pets of her own.

Use the stickers to dress the Dolls

Zoe

is brilliant at working
with wild horses and
loves riding. She is also
fascinated by reptiles.

Jack

has a passion for sea
creatures. He is a keen
birdwatcher and is never
without his binoculars.

Dolly Town

The Animal Rescue Dolls work at the Animal Sanctuary, in Dolly Town, home to all the Dolls. The Dolls work in teams to help those in trouble and are the very best at what they do, whether that's animal rescue, magical missions or caring for nature. Each day brings with it an exciting new adventure...

The **Shooting Star** train whisks the Dolls away on their missions.

The Dolls love to celebrate at the **Cupcake Café.**

Madame Coco's **Costume Emporium** has everything the Dolls might need.

Rose Theatre

The **Animal Sanctuary** is where the Animal Rescue Dolls work.

Bluebell Bookshop

Evergreen Sports Arena

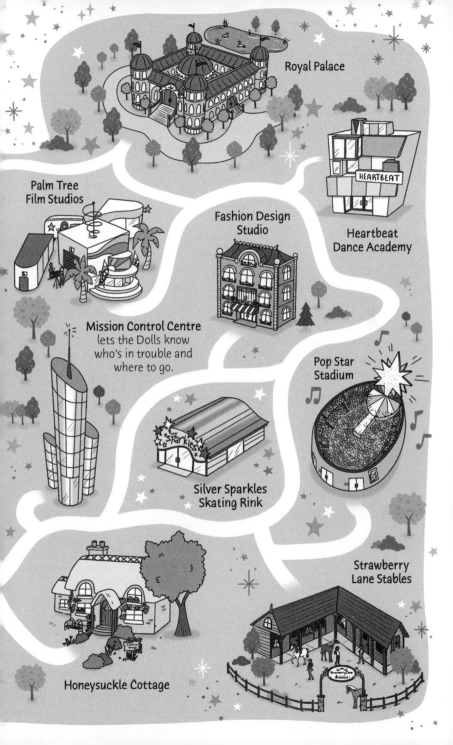

Royal Palace

HEARTBEAT

Heartbeat
Dance Academy

Palm Tree
Film Studios

Fashion Design
Studio

Mission Control Centre
lets the Dolls know
who's in trouble and
where to go.

Pop Star
Stadium

Silver Sparkles
Skating Rink

Strawberry
Lane Stables

Honeysuckle Cottage

Chapter One
Missing Puppy

It was winter in Dolly Town. Thick snow lay over the rooftops and a chill wind whistled down the streets. The Animal Rescue Dolls had been hard at work, caring for all the animals struggling with the cold.

"I've been leaving out scraps for the badgers," said Amelia.

"I've topped up the bird feeders," added Jack.

"And I've been melting the ice on the ponds," said Zoe, "to help all the creatures trapped beneath the surface."

"Excellent!" replied Amelia. "Now we just need to keep the Sanctuary as warm as

possible, so none of our rescue animals get cold."

"What about us though?" said Jack. "Alfie keeps hogging our heater!" They all laughed as they looked at Amelia's rescue dog, lying in front of the little radiator.

"Maybe we need hot chocolates to warm us up?" suggested Zoe.

"With marshmallows," said Jack. "And cream!"

"Great idea," said Amelia. "Let's go to the Cupcake Café."

Amelia put
Alfie in his pen
with a treat,
but as she
topped up his
water bowl,
everyone's mission
watches started to flash.

"Come in, Mission Control,"
said Zoe, tapping the symbol on
her watch. "We're all here. Has
something happened?"

"We've got an urgent mission
for you," said Mission Control.

The little sheepdog puppy at Bilberry Farm has gone MISSING. The farmer and her husband are out in the hills, checking on the sheep, and their son, Noah, is at home with his gran. He noticed the puppy missing about an hour ago and is worried she's got lost in the snow. Can you help?

"Of course," said Zoe. "We'll be there as soon as we can."

"Thank you," said Mission
Control. "Sending through the
mission details now."

Amelia reached for her screen,
just as the details came through.
The others all gathered round
to look.

MISSION LOCATION:

The Wild Isle

Stallion Falls

Rapido River

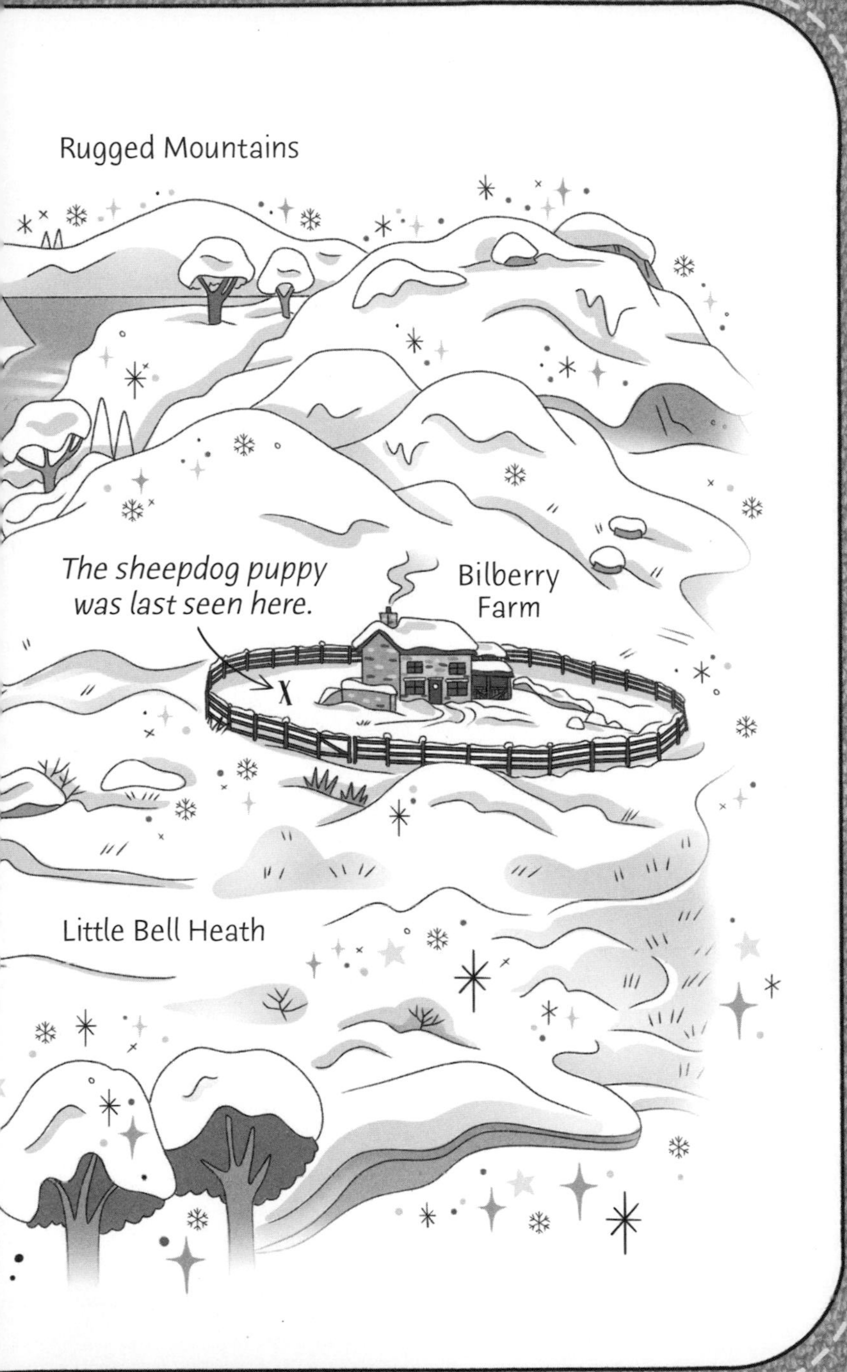

Rugged Mountains

The sheepdog puppy was last seen here.

X

Bilberry Farm

Little Bell Heath

Search for the Missing Puppy

Mission details:

The puppy was last seen an hour ago.

She has a thick coat to protect her from the snow, but is still at risk from the cold.

The temperature will drop when the sun goes down, so the puppy needs to be found quickly.

MOLLY, THE MISSING PUPPY

The sheepdog puppy is called Molly.
She is three months old and has a
fluffy black and white coat.

White face with
one black ear

Thick white
coat with black
patches

Shaggy tail

One black
front paw

"We're on the case," said Amelia. Then she turned to the others. "First stop…"

"Madame Coco's Costume Emporium," they chanted together.

The Dolls walked briskly across Dolly Town until they reached Madame Coco's. They made their way through the revolving doors into the welcoming warmth of the store, and headed straight for the famous glass elevator.

"Where would you like to go?" asked Jasper, the lift attendant, standing to attention in his gold-buttoned uniform.

"Floor number three, please," said Jack.

Of course. Step inside.

Jasper pressed
the button and
the lift whooshed
up, coming to a
stop with a gentle

TING!

When the
doors opened,
there was
Madame Coco,
dressed in a
stylish quilted
jacket.

"Hello, Madame Coco," said Amelia, smiling at her. "We've got an urgent mission to the Wild Isle. We need to rescue a puppy lost in the snow."

"Well, you've come to the right place," said Madame Coco. "I'll have your outfits ready in no time."

She turned as she spoke, a trail of assistants rushing to her side, and they circled the department floor, picking out the warmest possible clothes. "These will be perfect for trekking through snow," said Madame Coco, handing them to the Dolls.

Amelia's clothes

Chunky-knit
bobble hat

Pink and green
insulated jacket

Close-fitting
fleece gloves

Fleece-lined
tan boots

Mint green
waterproof trousers

Jack's clothes

Green and blue striped beanie

Powder blue mittens

Fleece-lined blue winter jacket

Lace-up trekking boots

Stretch trousers in 3-layer fabric

Zoe's clothes

Striped, elasticated headband

Two-tone lightweight jacket

Purple windproof and waterproof trousers

Matching orange mittens

Purple lace-up trekking boots

"For Amelia, we have a chic pink and green jacket – perfect for keeping out the cold. And a bobble hat in the softest wool.

For Jack, I've chosen a fleece-lined powder blue coat and these lovely green trousers.

And for you Zoe, a very stylish purple and orange jacket and trousers – and I couldn't resist this matching headband."

Then the Dolls' names flashed up above the changing rooms and they stepped inside.

When they stepped out again,
they were ready for their mission.

"Now," said Madame Coco, "time for your equipment. I've packed a dog first aid kit, blankets, torches, heat packs and rescue ropes."

"Thank you, Madame Coco," said Jack. "You think of everything."

"And last but not least…" Madame Coco went on, a twinkle in her eye,  and she handed them a tiny bag.

"It's sparkle dust," said Madame Coco, "from the Magic Dolls. The puppy's tracks could easily be covered by snow, but if you sprinkle this dust over the ground, it will reveal where the puppy has been."

"Oh! This will be a huge help," said Zoe.

"It's made out of hawthorn for hope, chamomile for patience, rosemary for remembrance and a little something extra for magic," said Madame Coco.

"Thank you, Madame Coco," said Amelia, placing it carefully in her pocket. "Now, we'd best get going."

With a final wave, the Dolls

stepped into the
lift once more.
The doors glided
shut and down
they whizzed.

TING!

Soon, they
were back on the
snowy streets.
"Time to call
the Shooting
Star!" said Jack,
tapping his watch.

Moments later, it
hove into view in a cloud of
glittering dust, snowflakes melting
softly against its sleek sides.

"Hello, Animal Rescue Dolls,"
said Sienna, the driver, smiling at
them from under her peaked cap.
"Where can I take you today?"

"The Wild Isle, please," said Amelia. "Bilberry Farm. We're off to rescue a missing puppy."

The Dolls stepped aboard and as the doors swished shut they looked at each other and smiled.

"It's Mission Go!" said Zoe.

"Wild Isle here we come!" they chanted together.

Chapter Two
Bilberry Farm

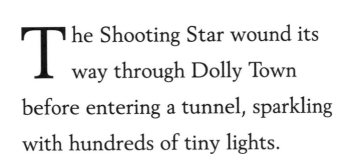

T he Shooting Star wound its way through Dolly Town before entering a tunnel, sparkling with hundreds of tiny lights.

With a

WHOOSH

it shot out the other side…and
into the Wild Isle.

"So much snow!" said Jack.
"I've never seen it like this before."

"Neither have I," added Zoe.
"Isn't it beautiful!"

She gasped to see the river had
become a ribbon of ice, gleaming
in the low winter sun.

The ground glittered in the sunshine and, in the distance, the snow-capped mountains rose up beneath an azure blue sky.

Then the Shooting Star began to head north, speeding over the heath, before drawing to a halt next to Bilberry Farm.

"Here you are, Dolls," said Sienna. "I'm glad you're kitted out for the snow!"

"We're prepared for everything," Zoe replied, grinning.

With those words, she stepped off the Shooting Star...straight into a snowdrift, right up to her middle.

"Oh my goodness," laughed Zoe. "I hadn't realized the snow was *this* deep!"

Then they all gave a last wave to Sienna, and trekked through the snow to the farmhouse.

A young boy stood in the doorway, smiling anxiously.

"Noah?" called Jack.

The boy nodded.

I'm so glad you're here. I'm worried about our pup, Molly.

"She's only three months old and we've not had her long and…"

"Slow down, Noah," said a voice, and a woman, with curly grey hair and bright eyes, appeared behind him. "Let's invite our guests into the warmth first."

She held the door open wide. "I'm Noah's gran," she added, with a smile, as she ushered the Rescue Dolls inside.

"Thank you," said Amelia. "Can you tell us when you last saw Molly and what happened?"

Noah took a deep breath. "My mum and dad set off this morning to check on the sheep, in case any were stuck in the snow. Molly was settled by the fire, and I went outside to get some more logs. But I must have left the door open because when I came back...Molly was gone!"

"We've searched the house and garden," his gran continued, "but there's no sign of her. It's not like her to hide away."

"And we can't call my parents," said Noah, "because there's no signal out in the hills. Even worse," his face fell, "I've found some of Molly's tracks going through a gap in the garden fence."

"Can you show us exactly where you saw the tracks?" asked Zoe.

"Come with me," said Noah, and he and his gran led the Dolls to the end of the garden. "I wanted to follow the tracks, but Gran said I couldn't go out in this weather…"

Jack picked up his binoculars and followed the trail. "It looks as if the puppy has headed west," he said. "We'd better set out immediately.

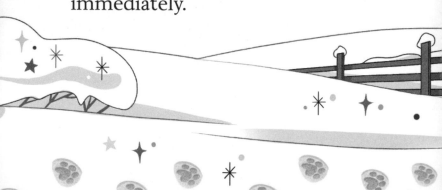

We need to find Molly before it gets dark and the temperature starts dropping."

"And it gets dark ever so early at this time of year," said Noah's gran.

Zoe could see Noah looking more anxious than ever. "Don't worry," she said. "We're on the case. And remember, Molly has a good, thick coat to keep her warm out there."

"It's going to be slow-going in this snow, though," said Amelia. "Do you have any horses we could borrow?"

"Noah's parents have ridden out on them," said Gran. "But you could take the huskies?"

"Huskies?" gasped Jack. He couldn't help grinning at the thought. "That would be a great help."

"And they might be able to follow Molly's scent too," suggested Zoe.

Amelia's eyes lit up. "Great idea," she said. "Noah, have you got anything that smells of Molly?

A toy that she likes, perhaps?"

Noah raced off and was soon back with a much-chewed toy. "Here you go," he said, handing it to Amelia. "The huskies are in the barn. I can take you there, if you like?"

"Yes please," said Amelia.

They followed Noah behind the house to the barn, where they were greeted by a chorus of friendly barks. Eight beautiful huskies, with thick coats, shining blue eyes and velvety pointed ears, rushed over to greet them.

"Meet Kara, Amur, Lena, Sasha, Kasha and Malchik," said Noah, pointing to each one in turn. "And these two are Miska and Siku. They're the lead dogs, so they go at the front." He handed Zoe a little bag of dog treats. "Do you need help setting up the sled?"

"It's okay," Amelia answered, reaching out to stroke the dogs.

"I've done lots of sledding before,
so I know how to do it."

She went round to Miska and
Siku and held out Molly's toy.
The dogs both leaned forward to
sniff. "Hopefully they'll
be able to pick up
her scent now."

Together, the Dolls hitched up
the dogs to the sled. Zoe and Jack
sat in the sled, while Amelia stood
at the back, her hands gripping
the handlebar.

"Ready!" Amelia called out to the
huskies. At once, they pricked up
their ears and stood to attention.

"Let's go!" she called, and, as she released the brake, the huskies began to run.

"Goodbye!" Zoe called to Noah. "And don't worry. We'll do everything we can to find Molly."

Then they were off, racing through the snow, the wind in their faces, following the little puppy's tracks.

Chapter Three

Into
the Wild

The huskies headed west,
pulling the sled behind them,
while the Dolls leaned this way
and that around the corners.
Soon they reached a frozen river,
covered in thick ice. They sped
over it and carried on, into the
foothills of the Rugged Mountains.

Zoe checked the compass on her mission watch. "We're still heading west," she said. "If we keep going this way, we'll reach Rapido River. I do hope the puppy hasn't come to any harm."

But as she spoke, the huskies veered suddenly to the right,

noses to the ground.

"Oh!" said Zoe. "Perhaps they're onto something."

"Yes," said Jack, peering at the ground. "The tracks are going this way – and look! Up ahead! There's a little cave in the side of the hill – maybe the puppy is in there!"

"Oh, I do hope so," said Zoe. "It's so cold and already the sky is getting darker. If Molly's in a cave, at least she'll be sheltered."

When they reached the cave entrance, Amelia called out, "Whoa!" and placed her feet on the brake. The huskies came to a swift halt, panting, their breath forming misty clouds in the cold air.

Jack got out to look, but as he neared the cave entrance, he let out a cry.

"What is it?" asked Zoe.

The entrance to the cave was low, and Jack had to crouch down on his hands and knees to peer inside.

"Be careful!" warned Zoe. "You don't want to come face to face with a wolf."

"No," said Jack, "but we have to find out if Molly is in there."

He crawled forward, calling Molly's name and shining his torch inside the cave.

Amelia and Zoe waited tensely, but when Jack reappeared, he looked downcast. "There's no sign of Molly. And no sign of a wolf, either," he added with a shaky laugh.

"Wait a moment!" said Zoe. "What's that?" She stepped forward and pulled some fur from a low branch by the cave.

She looked at it closely.

"It's Molly's, isn't it?" said Zoe, passing it to Amelia.

"Yes, that's definitely sheepdog fur," Amelia agreed.

"What do you think has happened here?" asked Zoe, her eyes wide.

"I don't know," said Jack. "But I don't like it one bit…"

Jack looked around, desperately scanning for more signs of Molly. "Hang on!" he said, his voice full of relief. "Over there. The puppy tracks carry on – can you see?"

"Yes!" said Amelia, craning forward. "Those are definitely the puppy tracks. Molly must have just

taken shelter in the cave. There's
no reason to think she was here at
the same time as the wolf, and the
wolf tracks aren't following hers.
I think we can hope for the best.
Back on the sled, everyone. Let's
find that puppy!"

Chapter Four

The Frozen River

The Dolls climbed back on board and Amelia gave the command for the huskies to start running again. Zoe kept a careful watch on the sky as it faded to a dusky pink. She knew they didn't have long until nightfall.

Soon, Rapido River came into

view, its icy surface gleaming
through the dusk. And as they
pulled up beside it, they saw the
tracks came to an abrupt end.

The Rescue Dolls climbed out
of the sled and Amelia turned it

carefully on its side, so the
huskies wouldn't pull it away.

As if knowing they wouldn't
be running again for a while,
the huskies lay down and began
rolling in the snow.

Zoe gave them some treats, then all three Dolls followed the last of the tracks down to the river.

"Maybe Molly crossed here," said Zoe. "That would explain why her tracks have stopped."

"But the ice has cracked and splintered," said Jack. "What if she's fallen in? She won't stand a chance in the freezing water."

Jack peered through his binoculars, his expression serious. "I can't see any tracks on the other side of the river…"

"If Molly did manage to cross the water," said Zoe, "then the huskies might not be able to pick up on her scent."

Amelia reached into her pocket and pulled out the bag of sparkle dust. "Now's the time to use this," she said. "Maybe there are more tracks, but they've just been covered by snow?"

The others
nodded hopefully,
and Amelia took out
a pinch of sparkle
dust. It glittered briefly
in the cold air before
floating out across the ground.
It lay there, sparkling in the snow…
but there was no sign of any tracks.

"I don't understand it," said
Jack. "The puppy can't have just
disappeared!"

"I know!" said Zoe. "Try
sprinkling it over the river."

Amelia took another pinch and cast it out over the river's frozen surface. They all gasped as they saw little paw prints glistening on the thin ice.

And that's when they heard it – a faint whine coming from further down river. "Could that be Molly?" wondered Amelia.

"I do hope so," said Zoe. "But it

sounds as if she's in trouble!"

"We'd best hurry on foot from here," said Amelia. "I'll tie up the huskies if you two fetch the rescue equipment."

"Will the huskies be okay?" asked Zoe.

Amelia nodded. "They'll be fine for a short while, and they're sheltered from the wind here."

As soon as they were ready, the Dolls made their way along the riverbank, following the thin, high whining sound.

"Oh look!" cried Jack, suddenly. "Thank goodness!"

For there, just beyond the bend in the river, was Molly, half camouflaged against the white of the landscape.

She was sitting on a rock in the middle of the river, clearly too

scared to move. Her eyes were wide and forlorn, and she was shivering too, her fluffy coat damp with snow.

"She must have ventured out onto the ice and then slipped downstream," said Zoe.

"And the ice is even thinner here," Jack pointed out. "I can see the river, flowing beneath its surface. How are we going to reach her?"

At the sight of them, Molly stepped off the rock, as if trying to reach them. But as soon as her paw touched the surface, the ice began to

splinter. Molly whimpered and retreated to her rock.

Amelia's brow was creased with worry. "She's been out a long time now and she's shivering. If we leave her much longer, she may get hypothermia and that can be dangerous. We need to get to her fast."

"But the ice here won't take our weight," said Jack, "and the water will be freezing."

"There must be a way," said Zoe. She started looking round,

and her eyes lit up as she spied some fallen branches under the trees.

"Let's use those," she said, pointing. "We can lay them like a bridge, from the riverbank to the rock. Even if the ice breaks, we'll be safe on the branches."

"We'll only need one of us to go," said Amelia. "I'm happy to do it, as I've had the most experience with dogs and puppies."

The others nodded and they all headed under the trees, looking for

branches that would be long
and strong enough to
take Amelia's weight.

"I think these should do," said
Jack, once he'd tied a few
branches together. Then they
began pushing them across the
river until the tops were resting
securely on the rock.

"Jack and I will hold onto this end, to keep the branches steady," said Zoe. "And we'll tie one of the rescue ropes around you as well. Then if anything goes wrong, we can pull you straight out of the river."

"I'm ready," said Amelia, once she was rigged up. "I'd better go across on my stomach. I don't fancy going through that ice…"

With those words, she lay herself down on the branches. Then she took a deep breath and started forwards across the frozen river…

Chapter Five

Icy
Rescue

J ack and Zoe held their breath
as they watched Amelia inch
her way along the branches.
She kept calling out to Molly,
soothing her with the sound of
her voice.

"Good girl," said Amelia. "Stay
there. I'm coming."

She had been worried the puppy might be scared of her, and try to escape across the ice. But from her whimpers of joy, wiggling hips and little wagging tail, she could tell Molly was overjoyed to see her.

But as she came closer,
Amelia saw just how much
Molly was shivering.

"Poor little pup. We've
got to you just in time,
haven't we?" she said,
reaching out for Molly
and drawing her close.

"You look like a little
wet cloud," she said, gently.

With relief, she realized Molly
was small enough to hold under
one arm, but it was still going to
be tricky getting back.

"I've got her," she called to
the others. "But there's no room

to turn. I'm going to have to do this backwards…"

"Just take your time," said Jack. "We're holding things steady here."

Slowly, carefully, Amelia began inching backwards. She could feel Molly shivering against her, but thankfully the puppy didn't squirm or try to get away. Amelia could feel how cold she was, too.

"Don't worry," she whispered. "We'll have you warm and dry soon."

But halfway across, more of the ice began to crack.

"You're nearly there," called
Jack. "Just keep going. We've
got you."

For a moment, Amelia looked

down at the splintering ice and the
dark waters beneath. As if sensing
danger, Molly began to struggle in
her arms.

"Don't panic, little one," said Amelia, holding her closer than ever.

She took another deep breath and kept going. And then, suddenly, she could feel Zoe and Jack reaching down for her, pulling them both to safety.

"You made it," said Zoe, her voice shaky with relief. "Well done, Amelia."

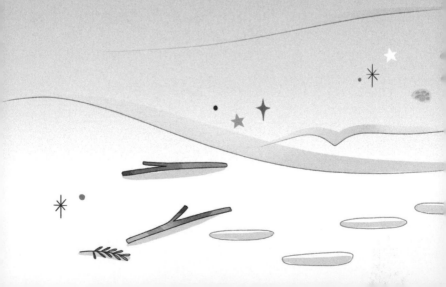

"And just in time, too," added Jack. "The dark is coming in fast now."

Looking up, Amelia could see the last of the light leeching from the sky.

"We're not quite in the clear yet," she replied. "I'm worried about how much Molly is shivering. Have you got the first aid kit?"

Jack swiftly handed it over.

As quickly as she could, Amelia wrapped Molly in a blanket and added a heat pack to warm her up.

Then she took her temperature.

"36 degrees," she told the others. "That's close to mild hypothermia. The sooner we get Molly home and warm the better, especially in this frosty air."

Without another word, they hurried back to the huskies, who welcomed them with wagging tails, eager to be off again.

The Dolls turned the sled and Amelia handed Molly to Jack. She was still wrapped up, snug in her fleecy blanket and making

little snuffly noises.

Jack and Zoe climbed on board while Amelia took up her position at the back.

"Ready?" Amelia asked the others. When they nodded, she lifted her foot from the brake and called out, "Let's go!"

As if sensing her urgency, the huskies leaped into action. "Hold fast," Amelia told the others.

Chapter Six

A Warm Welcome

There was no stopping this time, as the huskies leaped through the snow, their noses pointed for home. The sky was inky black, lit by shining stars.

"I think the huskies are as eager to get back as we are," laughed Zoe, watching in admiration as they ran together.

"And it's so much colder now,"
said Jack, hugging Molly close.
"I'm so glad we found her
before nightfall."

The sled sped across the frozen
ground and all the Dolls felt

grateful for Madame Coco's warm
clothes and woolly hats.

When they reached the farm,
Jack handed Molly to Amelia, who
hurried inside with her, while Jack
and Zoe took the huskies to the barn.

By the time Jack and Zoe had settled and fed the huskies, Molly was in a basket by the fire, lapping up some water and nibbling on a chew toy. Noah's eyes were shining with joy. Beside him, his parents and his gran all looked overjoyed at having Molly home again.

"Thank you so much for saving her," said Noah.

"What an adventurous puppy," said Gran, smiling down at her.

"I know," said Amelia. "I think

she must have got lost and then panicked, and just kept going! The good news is that her temperature is back to normal. You'll need to keep a close eye on her, checking

on her every ten minutes at first, to make sure it doesn't drop again. But I can't see any signs of frostbite and she's eating and drinking, which is good."

"She's much quieter than normal though," said Noah, still looking anxious.

"That's probably to be expected," replied his mum. "It's been a big day for a little puppy."

"And I'm sure she's going to be just fine," added Amelia, reassuringly.

"Well done, little Molly," said Zoe, bending down to stroke her. "Now she's dried out, I can feel how fluffy she is."

The others laughed while Jack

turned to see a small cat slinking into the room.

"Who's this?" he asked, as the cat wound between his legs.

"Oh, that's Milo!" said Noah. "Our pet cat. He and Molly haven't really learnt to be friends yet…"

Before he could finish speaking, Molly leaped out of her basket, barking, and Milo fled the room.

"Naughty puppy!" Noah scolded gently, scooping Molly up and putting her back in her basket.

"Well," said Noah's mum, "at least we can now say that Molly's back to her old self."

Everyone laughed, while Molly looked up at them expectantly, wagging her tail.

"On that note," said Amelia, giving Molly one last cuddle, "I think it's time for us to go. I need to get back to my own dog – and the other animals at the Sanctuary."

Jack tapped his watch to summon the Shooting Star while Noah and his family thanked the Dolls again and again.

With a final wave, the Dolls stepped out into the icy dark and made their way down the garden path towards the waiting train.

"Where would you like
to go?" asked Sienna. "The
Cupcake Café?"
"We'd love that," said Amelia,
"but we must check on the

animals first. Could you take
us to the Sanctuary?"

Sienna nodded and soon
they were whizzing across
the Wild Isle.

Then they entered the tunnel, which flickered with tiny lights.

WHOOSH

They were back in Dolly Town in no time, waving goodbye to Sienna and hurrying inside to check on all their animals.

Alfie gave Amelia a big welcome, barking excitedly and wagging his long tail.

"Good boy!" she said, bending down to give him a tummy rub.

Soon, though, there was a knock on the door.

"Come in!" called Zoe, and Maya, from the Cupcake Café, stepped into the room.

"Hello," she said, smiling. "A little bird told me you've been hard at work on the Wild Isle and could all do with some hot chocolates!"

She pulled a hamper into the room as she spoke, and lifted the lid to reveal cups of hot chocolate and plates piled high with treats.

"Oh, Maya!" said Jack, grinning. "You're the best."

"Will you join us?" said Amelia, as they laid everything out on the little table. "No, Alfie, I didn't mean you," she laughed, as he bounded towards the plate of cookies.

"I'd love to," said Maya, pulling up a stool.

"First," said Zoe, "a toast to Maya for keeping us going with her delicious food!"

To Maya!

"And to you!" said Maya. "For all the amazing work that you do."

"To the Animal Rescue Dolls!" they chanted together.

The End

Look out for new adventures with the **Magic Dolls**.

Visit **usborne.com**
to see more in this series.

The rescue mission and events in this book are entirely fictional and should never be attempted by anyone other than a trained professional.

Edited by Lesley Sims and Stephanie King
Designed by Hannah Cobley and Hope Reynolds
Additional design by Johanna Furst and Jacqui Clark
Additional illustrations by Heather Burns
Expert advice from Suzanne Rogers

First published in 2022 by Usborne Publishing Ltd.,
Usborne House, 83-85 Saffron Hill, London EC1N 8RT, England.
usborne.com Copyright © 2022 Usborne Publishing Ltd. UKE